The MILKWEED and Its World of Animals

The MILKWEED
and Its World
of Animals

By ADA and FRANK GRAHAM

Photographs by LES LINE

DOUBLEDAY & COMPANY, INC., GARDEN CITY, NEW YORK

This book is for
Jeannie, Susie, Joe, Tony and Dan,
who live in Milkweed Country.

The boy in the milkweed meadow is Michael Line,
the son of Mr. and Mrs. Les Line.

Designed by Laurence Alexander

Library of Congress Cataloging in Publication Data

Graham, Frank, 1925–
The milkweed and its world of animals.

SUMMARY: An introduction to ecology, focusing on a
single very common wild plant and its qualities which
affect a variety of animals that come in contact with it.
1. Meadow ecology—Juvenile literature.   2. Milkweed—Juvenile literature.   3. Insect-plant relation-
ships—Juvenile literature.   [1. Meadow ecology.
2. Ecology.   3. Milkweed.   4. Insect-plant relation-
ships]   I. Graham, Ada, joint author.   II. Title.
QH541.5.M4G7   574.5′264
ISBN 0-385-09932-0 Trade
0-385-09933-9 Prebound
Library of Congress Catalog Card Number 74–18801

Text copyright © 1976 by Ada and Frank Graham

Photographs copyright © 1976 by Les Line

FIRST EDITION

ACKNOWLEDGMENTS

The authors want to thank the many kind people
who shared their knowledge and extended their co-operation
to help to make this book possible. Especially helpful
in a variety of ways were Alyce M. Connor
of the Reference Department, and the entire staff of the
Childrens Department, of the Bangor, Maine, Public Library;
Viki Ferreniea of the New England Wild Flower Society;
Dr. Francis O. Holmes of Henniker, New Hampshire;
James Kienzler of the University of Maine; Michael Line
of Dobbs Ferry, New York; Dr. John C. Pallister of the
American Museum of Natural History; and Ronie St. Pierre
of Columbia, Maine.

1. AN INVADING ARMY

THERE IS A MEADOW in the countryside, bright with wild flowers. The meadow was once a pasture where cows grazed on warm summer days. The farm disappeared a long time ago. There have been many changes in the meadow in recent years, but it is still a beautiful place to visit and an exciting place to explore.

The meadow used to be almost completely covered with a carpet of red-top grass, a favorite food of cows. Wild flowers such as daisies and meadowsweet grew among the grass. The grass and the wild flowers are still there, but at the edges of the old field many woody shrubs and trees are beginning to move in. The cows once trampled or nibbled away these large plants before they had a chance to grow tall and strong. Now, like an invading army, the aspens and pine trees are beginning to take over the meadow.

The milkweed meadow.

Anyone who explores there can see how large the meadow used to be. It was enclosed by a stone wall. But now the wall is grown over with bushes and small trees. It is hard to find it. Nature is taking back the land that the farmer once cleared. The meadow grows a little smaller every year.

In the middle of the old field, not reached yet by the invading trees, is a stand of tall plants topped by clusters of pale pink and lavender flowers. There are many insects around these plants—butterflies, bees, flies and day-flying moths. Mice live in the grass nearby. The plants belong to one of the most familiar and yet most remarkable families in the world, the milkweeds.

There are over two thousand kinds of milkweed in the world. Most of the milkweeds grow in Africa. Other kinds grow in South America. Because they have many uses, milkweeds have been planted in Europe and Asia where they do not grow naturally. They are used for food, medicine and as fibers for making cloth.

There are over a hundred kinds of milkweed plants that grow naturally in North America. Indians used the milkweed flowers and tender young pods in their stews of buffalo meat. The early settlers sent milkweed seeds back to England so that they could be grown there, just as they sent back corn and potatoes.

Different kinds of milkweed plants grow wherever it is not too cold, from the Gulf of Mexico into southern Canada. Many kinds grow as vines in the desert. Some grow in swamps. Around the Gulf of California milkweeds grow as woody shrubs in thickets that are more than one hundred years old.

One of the most BEAUTIFUL kinds of American milkweed is called the butterfly weed. It has brilliant orange-red flowers. A hundred years ago people in Holland got seeds from America, grew the colorful flowers, and sent them back here to exhibit at a large fair. Then Americans began to realize how beautiful these wild flowers are. People have grown butterfly weed in their flower gardens ever since!

Milkweed sprouting in the meadow.

But for many of us the most familiar plant is the common milkweed. It grows in many places in the eastern and central United States. It is, in fact, called a weed because it is so common. You will see it from your car as it grows by the side of the highway. You will sometimes see large patches of it growing in the fields that you pass. You will also see milkweed plants as you walk through vacant lots in town. The common milkweed likes all these dry places.

The common milkweed has grown for many years in the meadow where cows once grazed. Hundreds of plants form a little world in themselves. You see their pretty flowers as you pass but you probably miss all the things that are going on. If you explore this little world you will see that it is a kind of zoo, made up of tiny animals of many different kinds.

2. MONARCH OF THE MEADOW

THE MILKWEED PLANTS began to appear in the meadow in spring. They were just tiny sprouts at first, pushing their way up through the surrounding grass. Each leaf was wrapped lengthwise around the stem. In this position only the fuzzy white underside of the leaf could be seen.

Some of the plants had sprouted from the seeds of last year's milkweed. Other plants had sprouted from the dense milkweed root system that has lived underground in this meadow for many years. The root system would send up many more milkweeds, but in some places the red-top grass grows too densely for it.

The leaves of the young milkweed plant open in pairs. They grow opposite each other on the stem. Each day the milkweed grows a little taller. People come and pick the young milkweed plants while they are still moist and tender. It is a wild vegetable and they eat the stems like asparagus and boil the leaves like spinach.

Other living things look for young milkweed plants too. The air over the meadow is splashed with color. Reddish-brown and black butterflies flutter and dip in flight over the young milkweed plants. The plants are still only a few inches high. The leaves unfold themselves from the stem. The fuzzy white undersides are like velvet to our touch. But it is the dark green upper surface that we most often see. It is decorated with a pattern of slender veins. The leaves are long and narrow, coming to a tip at the point. The butterflies do not stop at the dandelions, the hawkweeds or the other plants of the meadow. The milkweeds have sent them an age-old message. These are monarch butterflies and they have come to the milkweed plants to lay their eggs.

The monarchs are often called milkweed butterflies. Their lives are bound up with milkweed plants. They come to the plants every year when the leaves are soft and young. The female butterfly lands on a leaf. She presses her body against the soft green surface, usually the underside of the leaf, and lays one white egg. The egg is the size of the head of a pin.

The wet, sticky egg dries quickly in the air and sun. It sticks to the leaf. The butterfly flies to another milkweed leaf and lays another egg.

On sunny days in spring the butterfly moves from one of the soft dark leaves to another, from one small growing milkweed plant to another, from one flowering meadow to another. She never deposits more than one egg on a leaf. Before she is finished, she sometimes lays as many as four hundred eggs. By selecting only the milkweed plants, she makes sure that many of her young will hatch and become beautiful reddish-brown and black butterflies like herself.

Milkweed leaves grow opposite each other on the stem.

The monarch butterfly leaves a white egg on a leaf.

When you walk through the meadow stop at one of the small young milkweed plants. Look closely at the leaves. Turn them over gently to where the fine white hairs form a whitish mat on the underside. Among the fuzzy growth you may find one of the tiny white eggs—a reminder of the large butterfly that visited it only a day or two before. Remember this plant. If you return to it later you will see the surprising new creature that has made the milkweed plant its home.

3. "DON'T EAT ME!"

THE MILKWEED PLANT grew quickly in the warm sun. Life was also stirring in the tiny egg that was stuck to the fuzzy underside of one of its leaves. A caterpillar was forming inside. Two or three days after the egg was laid the caterpillar of the monarch butterfly chewed its way through the egg shell and crawled out onto the leaf.

The caterpillar didn't look anything like a monarch butterfly. It looked like a little worm with a dark head. It was very small and it was also very hungry. The first thing it did was to eat what was left of the egg.

Now it becomes clear why the monarch butterfly laid her egg at this time and on this leaf. She laid her egg when the milkweed plant was still very young. The leaf was moist and

tender, not dry and tough as an old leaf would be. The baby caterpillar was able to begin feeding on the leaf.

The caterpillar ate rapidly. It chewed holes along the edge of the leaf. After a while a faint milky white liquid could be seen oozing at places where the caterpillar had chewed through the vein. This milky substance runs all through the stem and the leaves of the milkweed and gives the plant its name.

The monarch caterpillar had an advantage over other kinds of baby insects whose parents laid their eggs on other plants. The milky liquid in the leaves is very bitter. The milkweed caterpillar seems to like the taste, but larger animals do not. Rabbits eat many of the other tender shoots in the field but not milkweed. Cattle, deer, woodchucks and other grazing animals avoid the milkweed too. They eat different plants, and the eggs and baby insects on them get eaten up too. But the monarch caterpillar has a better chance to survive. The larger animals can't stand the taste of the plant it lives on! That may be one reason why monarch caterpillars and butterflies are so common.

The baby caterpillar kept on eating milkweed leaves. Like the plant, it was growing fast. But an insect is different from human beings and dogs and cats. Its skeleton is on the *outside* of its body. It doesn't stretch as it grows. The baby caterpillar soon outgrew its skin.

Before the caterpillar could grow any more it had to get rid of its old skin. It began to spin a silk carpet. It put its head close to the leaf. From a spinner on its lower lip it began to lay down a mat of silken thread. The caterpillar moved its head from side to side. The silk formed a carpet on the leaf.

The caterpillar has hooks on its legs. It hooked these legs into the silk. Then it took in air through tubes in its body, just as we would puff up our chest by breathing deeply. In this effort the old skin began to split. The caterpillar held itself tightly to the leaf while pushing its body upward. It wriggled to free itself. The old skin split some more. Finally the caterpillar struggled out of the skin head-first, dressed in the new covering it had grown beneath the old skin.

This tiny caterpillar doesn't resemble the large monarch butterfly it will become.

The caterpillar, hanging from a milkweed leaf, has three pairs of legs and five pairs of prolegs. The horns, at each end of its body, are called whiplashes.

We can see the caterpillar much better now. It is over an inch long and still growing. It is brightly colored, white and greenish yellow with prominent black bands. At each end of the body it has two long threadlike horns that are called whiplashes. Like all insects it has three pairs of legs attached to its middle section. It also has five pairs of prolegs which are very fleshy and have tiny hooks.

The caterpillar does not need wings. It walks on its many legs from leaf to leaf on the milkweed plant, eating as it goes. That's all the caterpillar does—eat and eat, and grow and grow. Four times during the two weeks that it is a caterpillar it must shed its skin so it can grow.

The little caterpillar chews and chews and grows and grows.

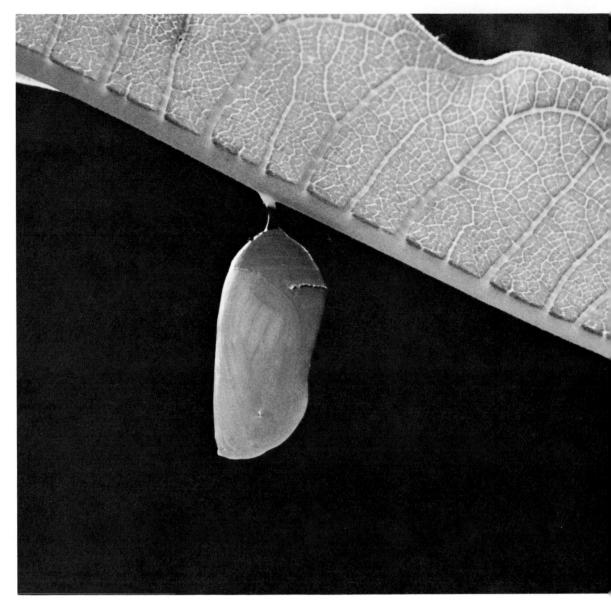

After two weeks of life as a caterpillar, the monarch forms a chrysalis around its body and hangs from a milkweed leaf.

Some of the caterpillars, of course, do not live to become butterflies. They are killed and eaten by wasps or other insects. But an insect like the monarch caterpillar *is* what it eats. As it eats the milkweed leaves, the bitter milky liquid becomes a part of its own body. Birds that eat other caterpillars usually leave monarchs alone.

In the chrysalis, it develops into its adult form and emerges as a butterfly.

The monarch will carry this bitter fluid in its body all its life. Even when it becomes a butterfly it will taste bad. This fact has interested scientists for many years. Scientists have fed monarchs to birds in captivity. If the bird had never seen a monarch before, it would eat the butterfly. But it vomited the butterfly right away. The bird would never eat another monarch. Even if the monarchs had been raised on cabbage plants instead of on milkweeds the bird also refused to eat them. It knew from its color that it was likely to taste bad.

The monarch's bright color becomes a signal: "Don't eat me. I taste awful!" The color of the monarch butterfly's wings—orange bordered with black bands—protects it from birds and other predators.

There is another common butterfly called the viceroy. The viceroy is about the same size as the monarch, with orange wings bordered with black. The viceroy has an extra black line on its hind wing, but otherwise it is so much like the monarch that birds and other insect-eaters do not notice the difference. They avoid eating viceroys too.

Sometimes it pays to have a look-alike in nature.

4. A SCIENTIST IN THE MEADOW

AS THE MILKWEED PLANTS and the monarch caterpillars grow, other plants and animals are growing around them. Plants are taking food from the soil. All the animals in the meadow, large and small, depend on the plants to manufacture food and turn it into energy that they can use. Some animals are eating the plants. Other animals are eating the plant-eating animals.

The meadow, we can already see, is not simply a collection of separate plants and animals. Each kind depends on another. The meadow is a community of living things.

Even the red-top grass plays an important part. Its dense root system holds the soil together. It grows so thickly that it slows down the growth of trees and shrubs. This keeps the meadow open so that milkweeds can get the sunshine they need to grow. And to the milkweeds come the monarchs and other animals that depend on them.

Jim is a scientist who comes to the meadow to study this community. Like many other scientists, he is interested in finding the paths taken by energy as it changes shape and form.

The energy from which living things draw their strength originally comes from the sun. The plants of the meadow are able to make use of the sun's energy. Their leaves manufacture food with the help of sunlight. Energy, in the form of food, is passed on, like water in pipes, through tiny tubes to the rest of the plant. Insects and other animals that feed on the plant take in this energy. If these animals are eaten by larger animals, the energy is passed along once more.

And so the energy is kept moving among all the things that live in the meadow, as one of them eats another. Jim is interested in finding out how each living thing plays its part in changing this energy into different forms of food.

There is only so much energy available in the meadow. It must be kept moving between all the things that live there. Jim is interested in finding out how each living thing plays its part in changing this energy through different forms of food.

How can a scientist trace such a complicated picture? There are so many plants and so many insects in the meadow. They are always changing, like the caterpillar turning milkweed leaves into growing caterpillar tissue. Jim cannot follow all the changes at once. So he makes use of modern science. He uses radioactive materials to do the job for him.

If you walk past the meadow, you will see a strange sight. Jim wears a white coat and plastic gloves and a special badge. Radioactive materials are dangerous if they are used carelessly or in large amounts. Nuclear bombs give off radioactive materials when they explode. But X-ray machines also give off these materials. They do not harm us in that case because they are used in such small amounts.

"I put radioactive materials in milkweed plants," Jim says. "But the amount I use is so small that you would have to eat seventy-five milkweed plants to get as much radiation as you would from one X ray at the dentist."

Nevertheless, Jim needs permission from the United States Atomic Energy Commission to use the radioactive material. He wears a badge to show he has a permit from the commission. He wears gloves and a white coat to protect his hands and his clothes from the material. He works with radioactive material because with sensitive instruments it can be traced as it moves through living things.

Jim chooses a number of milkweeds and other plants to study in the meadow. He makes a small slit in the stem of each plant. With a syringe he injects some water into the stem. There is radioactive material in the water. Then he puts glue over the slit he made so that no insects can crawl into the stem.

The water and radioactive material have entered the sap of the plant. They are carried wherever the sap goes. Jim wants to follow that sap and see what happens to it.

During the summer he returns to the meadow many times to collect various plants and animals.

"I bring a net," Jim says. "I sweep it through the grass to collect insects of every kind. Then I take them back to the laboratory with the plants I collect. I put the plants and animals, one at a time, into a metal container. Then I put the container into a very sensitive machine called a gas-flow geiger counter. The machine tells me exactly how much radiation each plant and insect contains."

In this way, Jim has been able to find out where the radiation goes after he has put it into the plants he selected in the meadow. Sometimes he finds the radiation in the flowers of another milkweed plant that he did not inject. Then he knows that the radioactive materials went down the stem of the plant and into its roots.

The root system of a large patch of milkweed plants is very complicated. Many new plants sprout from the underground roots. Jim's research shows that fluids from one plant pass out of the stem into the roots and then up the stem of another plant to its flowers. The different plants are really connected.

Jim also finds radiation in the insects that live on the plants. These insects receive the radiation from eating the

The plants of the milkweed patch are all connected by their root systems.

leaves and other parts of the plants. Jim is able to tell which insects are eating the plants. The amount of radiation in their bodies also tells him if they eat mostly milkweeds, or eat many other kinds of plants.

He also finds radiation in spiders and insects that do not eat plants. They take in the radiation by feeding on plant-eating insects. Spiders that eat a lot of these insects contain lots of radiation.

"It isn't easy to make a study like this," Jim says. "I have been collecting insects for a long time. When I was a boy the Smithsonian Institution in Washington paid me to collect fireflies. The scientists were making an experiment and needed lots of fireflies. But there are so many insects around the plants in the meadow that I still don't know all of their names."

Jim must know the names of all the insects so that he can list them in his reports. He is able to look some of them up in books. But he must take other insects to experts so that they can look at them.

Jim's experiments helped him to see how energy was constantly moving through the different living things in the meadow. They showed him something else too. As he collected them, he realized how many families of insects lived in the milkweed colony. It gave him much pleasure, as it does other visitors to the meadow, to look at these strange creatures closely and try to put them into their proper families.

5. WHAT IS AN INSECT

ONE DAY A DIFFERENT kind of caterpillar came to the milkweed plant. It was the caterpillar of the milkweed tiger moth. It did not look at all like the monarch caterpillar that was feeding on a leaf just above it. The newcomer was yellow, black and white. It had bunches of hair growing out in tufts all over its body. Even though it didn't look like the monarch caterpillar, the birds stayed away from it too. By eating milkweed leaves, it also tasted bad to insect-eaters.

The tiger moth caterpillar is very different from the monarch caterpillar, but at the same time, it has much in common with it. As we watch the life in the milkweed patch we will find many different insects. Before we look closely at some more of these creatures, let us see what an insect is.

The caterpillar of the milkweed tiger moth has colorful tufts.

The remains of insects have been found in rocks that are more than 300 million years old. The word insect itself comes from the Latin word "incised." This refers to the insect's body, which is deeply cut or "incised" between each of its three parts—the head, the thorax and the abdomen.

As we saw in the case of the monarch caterpillar, an insect wears its skeleton on the outside. It has no bones. Its tough outer covering shapes its body, just as our bony inner skeleton shapes ours.

An insect's body is fitted with parts that allow it to walk, jump, dig, fly or swim. All insects have six legs, three on each side of the body. Each leg has a claw or a hook so that the insect can hold on to things. Some insects, like flies, have sticky pads on their feet and can walk up a wall or across a ceiling.

Most insects have wings when they grow into adults. These wings, which are very thin, are attached to the middle section of the body, the thorax. Usually an insect has two pairs of wings, as a butterfly or a beetle does.

Insects have different kinds of mouths. Caterpillars have jaws for chewing, but these jaws move sideways instead of up and down as ours do. Other insects, such as mosquitoes, have mouths for sucking the juices from plants or the blood from animals. A butterfly has a long hollow tongue. It is usually curled up under its head. When it wants to drink the nectar from flowers it uncurls its tongue and pushes it down into the flower.

Adult insects have a pair of antennae between their eyes. We call them feelers because they are very sensitive to the touch. An insect uses its antennae to investigate the world around it. It feels things with its antennae, and some insects even use them to smell or "hear."

Most insects have two large eyes, one on each side of the head (sometimes *two* on each side). Some insects also have small simple eyes on top of the head. Insects can see in many directions at the same time, but they do not see things as sharply as we do.

Some insects, such as grasshoppers, have their ears located on their knees. Other insects pick up sound vibrations through their antennae. Others, such as honeybees and many moths and butterflies, are deaf.

Insects have a sense of taste just as we do. Some insects are able to taste with their antennae, too, so that they do not have to put food in their mouths to see if it is good. The honeybee and some butterflies have taste buds in their feet. They can just walk on food and tell if they like it or not!

A moth is one of the many insects that comes to milkweed.

No one knows exactly how many kinds of insects there are in the world. Some scientists say there are 700,000. Others think there may be as many as three million kinds or more. How can we even begin to tell them apart?

The only way to begin to sort them out is to put them in families or orders. There are so many kinds of insects in each order that some scientists are experts in only one order. Other scientists might say "John is a butterfly man," or "Louise is a beetle woman."

The insects in a single family or order have many things in common. Most of the orders are given scientific names that describe the kind of wings that are common to the insects belonging to that group. The butterflies and moths belong to the "scaly-winged" order. The flies are called "two-winged." The stink bugs are called "half-winged," and the beetles are called "sheath-winged."

An insect has two antennae, six legs, and a "skeleton" on its outside.

6. THE LIFE OF THE MILKWEED BEETLE

AS SUMMER COMES ON, more creatures of all kinds climb or fly to the milkweed plants. Chewing busily on a leaf is a red insect, spotted with black, and having very long antennae. It is called the red milkweed beetle and it spends its entire life on or very close to milkweed plants.

This beetle likes to eat the tenderest leaves. It often climbs to the top of the plant where the new leaves are just coming out. It starts chewing at the tip of the leaf and eats its way back toward the end, leaving only a wide U-shaped strip when it is finished. If there are flower buds on the plant, the milkweed beetle eats them too. Later on it will eat the flowers.

The adult beetles lay their eggs in the ground beneath milkweed plants. When the young beetles hatch they are very different from the pretty, shiny adults. They begin life as small white grubs, almost without legs and with round heads.

Many kinds of insects go through such a series of changes in their lives. From the egg they hatch into grubs or, like the monarch, into a caterpillar. Then after eating hungrily and

The red milkweed beetle has climbed to the tip of the leaf to begin eating.

growing rapidly, they spin a cocoon and go through a period of change during which they are called pupae. This is the period when the insect remains hidden and very still while great changes take place in its body. They come out of the cocoon as winged adults. Scientists call this life story "complete metamorphosis."

The beetle grubs begin feeding on milkweed roots. Often they dig tunnels through the soil in which they travel from one set of roots to another. Like other beetles, these grubs have strong mouths. They are able to bore through the plant's roots. They may spend the winter as grubs underground, building cells in which they stay warm and dry.

When it is full grown a grub tunnels near the surface and pupates in a cocoon or pupal cell. It comes out of the pupal cell in the early summer, changed into the familiar red milkweed beetle. It is about a half-inch long. It belongs to the family of long-horned beetles, and its antennae may be longer than its body.

The milkweed beetle has a scientific name even longer than its antennae. It is called *tetraopes tetraophthalmus,* which means "four-eyed four-eyes." This name refers to the fact that the beetle's large compound eyes are divided so that it seems to have two large eyes on each side of its head.

The compound eyes of insects are very special organs. They are made up of many tiny lenses. Each lens forms part of the picture for the insect. The optic nerve puts all the separate images together into one picture.

One scientist has compared this process to a stained-glass window. The window is made up of many small pieces of different-colored glass that, when all put together, form a single picture.

Insects see colors differently than we do. Those, like the milkweed beetle that feed on leaves, have eyes that are usually more sensitive to green, but less sensitive to other colors.

Because it feeds on milkweed leaves the milkweed beetle tastes just as bitter as the monarch. Its bright red and black coloring warns birds and other predators to stay away.

7. PLAYING DEAD

LOOK AT THE PICTURES on pages 32 and 33. The insects shown there are both leaf beetles that feed on milkweeds throughout a large part of the United States. Most insects of one kind look so much alike that you cannot tell one individual from another. But if you look closely you can see that the markings on the backs of these two leaf beetles are slightly different. Leaf beetles are so pretty and so various in their markings that some people make collections of them.

There are so many beetles that some scientists spend their lives trying to learn about them alone. There may be as many as a quarter of a million kinds of beetles in the world. Twenty-five thousand kinds live in the United States alone. In fact, there are more beetles than any other kind of insect. The scientific name for the order of beetles, *coleoptera,* means "sheath-winged." Beetles have two kinds of wings. One pair is light and thin for flying. The other pair is hard and shiny and is folded over the flying wings to protect them, like a sheath.

The leaf beetle's shiny back has big black spots.

Beetles have always had special meanings for human beings. Scarab beetles were sacred to the ancient Egyptians, who pictured them in their art as symbols of everlasting life. Museums keep collections of the beetles carved by ancient artists.

The Greeks and Romans ate the grubs of beetles. Roasted beetles are still favorite foods of the people in many parts of the world today, including China, Africa, South America and

The spots on this leaf beetle's back are slightly different.

the West Indies. People who eat them say they taste like the bone marrow of beef.

The leaf beetle that feeds on milkweed belongs to a different family than the red milkweed beetles. The leaf beetle looks like a big ladybird beetle, nearly a half-inch long. It, too, is a beautiful insect, its shiny orange back ornamented with black markings. Its antennae are much shorter, however, and its eyes are not as large as those of the red milkweed beetle. In fact, the leaf beetle's head looks as if it has been pushed down into the thorax or middle part of its body so that its small eyes are almost covered up.

There are many kinds of leaf beetles besides the one that feeds on milkweed. Most of them eat wild plants. But one of them, the Colorado potato beetle, has now become a serious pest. It used to eat wild plants mainly, such as nightshade. When the potato was brought to the United States for use as a food crop, the Colorado potato beetle took a liking to it and now causes great damage to potato plants.

But the leaf beetles in the pictures here cause no damage to man's crops. They are content to stay on milkweed. Like the other insects that feed on this plant, this beetle is protected from many predators because of its bad taste. Just in case a predator does not get the warning signal from its bright coloring, the beetle has another defense when it is attacked. It simply lets go of the milkweed leaf, falls to the ground and curls up as if dead.

The next time you see a leaf beetle on milkweed, poke it gently and see what happens.

8. THE MILK THAT HEALS

THE MILKWEED PLANTS are still growing in the meadow. Some of them are taller than a boy or a girl. Buds are swelling on all of the plants. A few have already burst open, revealing the pale lavender and pink flowers inside.

But some of the plants already look worn and ragged. Many insects have come to feed on their leaves, tearing their edges or leaving gaping holes. Here and there the plants are spotted and stained white by the milky juice that has seeped out where the insects have chewed into the leaves or stems. It is as if the plants are bleeding a pure white blood!

You can examine this sticky white juice that gives the plant its name. Break or cut the stem. Blot its broken end and then you will see the "milk" seeping from the dark green fibers that circle the cavity in the center of the stem. Rub some of it on your fingers. When it dries it becomes sticky and rubbery.

The milkweed has grown taller than a boy.

The sticky white juice runs down the stem.

According to some old stories, Indian children once collected the milkweed juice, let it dry and used it as a kind of chewing gum. A camper who found a tear in his air mattress used the juice as a glue to repair the leak. During World War II, when our government needed replacements for many materials it could not find, it experimented with milkweed juice as a substitute for rubber.

Milkweed juice has never become successful as a substitute for glue or rubber because it cannot be gathered in large enough quantities to make it economical. But it serves a very useful purpose for the plants themselves. When the plant is slit or punctured, the juice seeps out around the wound. When it hardens, it seals up the wound and prevents further damage to the plant.

Plants, in fact, are generally filled with various saps and juices. Many kinds of insects, instead of chewing the leaves or other parts of the plants, have mouth parts that fit them for piercing the stem or other parts and sucking the juices.

Planthoppers like to suck the juices of milkweeds. They belong to the order of insects called true bugs. They are very quick, hopping from plant to plant. A planthopper's lower lip is drawn out into a long beak that covers its sharp jaws. The jaws pierce the plant and fit together into a tube through which the insect drinks the plant's juices.

Planthoppers suck the juices of milkweeds.

9. ANT-COW

THE MILKWEED PATCH is now a small jungle. Caterpillars crawl up the stems, looking for tender leaves. Red milkweed beetles chew busily at the tip of a long leaf. Planthoppers leap from plant to plant. In the midst of all this activity there is a colony of insects clinging to a milkweed leaf as motionlessly as barnacles holding fast to a rock at the edge of the sea.

This colony is made up of curious animals called scale insects. Like the planthoppers, they suck the juices from plants. Yet they never move once they have reached the leaves on which they choose to feed. They are called scale insects because the females cover themselves with scales or plates of wax, which they make in their own bodies.

These tiny insects gather in large numbers on various plants and often destroy them. The males have one pair of wings and look like gnats. But they have no mouths and cannot eat! The females do all the damage. When they are young they have wings too, and they fly from plant to plant. Once they become adults, they settle down on a leaf for the rest of their lives. Many of them lose their legs, their wings, and their eyes.

Checking leaves for colonies of aphids in the milkweed meadow.

Protected by their coat of waxy scales, the females attach their mouths to the leaf and begin sucking its juices. Most kinds of scale insects even lay their eggs right there on the leaf. Some lay them under their bodies, while others keep the eggs within their bodies until they hatch. Then the young scale insects crawl out alive.

Even a scale insect colony is likely to be a busy place. On many of the milkweed leaves, other insects are often carrying on their own lives among the scale colony, or close to it. On one leaf there is another colony of sucking insects called aphids. Scientists say that aphids lead one of the strangest and most complicated lives of any creatures in the world.

We know that this leaf is special just by looking at it. It is marked with shiny white patches of dried liquid. Hundreds of aphids are moving about on the leaf. Some of them are a quarter of an inch long, others are smaller. Each aphid has a small head and thorax, and a large pear-shaped abdomen. Some have wings, colored green or brown, but most of the aphids are wingless. Walking about among the aphids, like keepers, are large black carpenter ants.

People who grow plants say that aphids are pests. They suck all the juices from leaves and the plants die. Scientists who study them say that aphids are a big problem too because they are so hard to keep track of. One of the problems for both plant growers and scientists is that aphids are so good at multiplying.

"It's lucky for us that lots of birds and insects eat aphids," a scientist says. "Otherwise, if there was enough food for them, the aphids hatched from one egg in the spring would have enough descendants by the fall to equal the weight of the earth."

This is how aphids multiply so fast:

Female aphids hide their eggs in the fall in cracks in the bark of trees or other protected places. The eggs stay there all winter unless they are found and eaten by chickadees and other birds. The young hatch, usually in the spring, when leaves begin to grow. These young aphids are all females. There are no males.

A carpenter ant walks across a colony of motionless scale insects.

Within a few days the female aphids produce young aphids of their own. Males do not fertilize the mother aphids. Because there is no contact between the sexes, as is usually the case in producing the young, the process is called asexual.

All of the young in this new generation are wingless females. These females soon produce their own generation of wingless females. A number of generations are produced in this way on the same plant. Finally, a generation of winged females is produced. By this time the plant is crowded with aphids. They have sucked most of the juices from it. Its leaves are curled and withered.

The winged females fly away to another plant. There they start a new colony. The colony is still composed of females. They give birth to more wingless female aphids. There is no need for these new generations to have wings because they are living on a fresh plant with plenty of food. They do not have to fly to other plants.

After many generations of wingless females the summer comes to an end. The plants begin to die. Now, at last, a generation hatches that is composed of both males and females. They mate in the fall. The females deposit their oval black eggs in safe places for the winter. The next spring this cycle begins all over again. No wonder aphids present problems for plant growers and scientists!

Carpenter ants look on aphids in a much better light. Aphids have a special way of feeding. Ants take advantage of this and keep herds of aphids just as ranchers keep herds of cattle. In fact, aphids are often called "ant-cows."

During the summer, aphids feed hungrily on leaves. Plant juices are mostly water. To get enough food from them, aphids must drink large quantities of juices. As they suck in the juices they filter them, keeping the food and getting rid of the extra water.

The aphids pump out the water in drops through a tiny hole in the abdomen called an anus. These drops of water have been sweetened by sugar in the aphids' bodies. This sweet liquid is called honeydew. Honeydew falls on the leaves where the aphids are feeding. It dries into shiny, sugary patches.

A carpenter ant tends a herd of aphids.

Carpenter ants love honeydew. These large ants get their name from their habit of making tunnels in old trees, wooden poles and the timbers of houses and barns. They do not eat wood as termites do. They make their nests in tunnels and lay their eggs there.

Carpenter ants often let aphids produce their food. They gather around aphid colonies to collect honeydew. In many cases they tend whole colonies of aphids. They herd them like cattle, moving the wingless aphids from one leaf "pasture" to another when the aphids run out of food. They protect the aphids, which are weak and defenseless, against their enemies. When the weather is bad, the ants sometimes move aphids into their own shelters.

Carpenter ants deserve their name of "the dairymen of the insect world."

10. OUR FRIEND, THE BEETLE

Ladybug! Ladybug! Fly away home.
Your house is on fire, and your children will burn.

THE LADYBUG, WHICH is often called the ladybird beetle, is one of the most familiar insects in the world. Everyone knows a ladybug, and everyone seems to like them. While there are some people who are afraid of most insects or do not like them, the ladybug is looked on as a friend.

The ladybug, with its bright orange or red back marked with large black spots, is a pretty insect. But there are other pretty insects that are not looked on as friends. For many hundreds of years people in different lands have looked on ladybug beetles as something special because of the help they have given them in fields and orchards. Even though these tiny insects look harmless, they are fierce enemies of pesky creatures such as aphids and scale insects. In Europe the people thought so highly of these beetles that they named them in honor of Our Lady, the Virgin Mary.

The poem at the head of this chapter was composed long ago in Europe. After the growing season the vines of hop plants were burned so that aphids would not hide their eggs in them during the winter. The people knew that often the lady-bug larvae, or young, also lived in the vines so that they could feed on aphids. The poem was a warning to the ladybug that her "house" was burning and that her young would be destroyed.

Sometimes the ladybug reminds us of a tiny turtle. It is flat on the bottom. Its "shell" is really its hard sheathlike wings which, in beetles of many kinds, cover the soft flight wings. The different kinds of ladybugs can often be identified by the number and arrangement of the spots on their wings. Some ladybugs have only two spots, others may have as many as fifteen.

Ladybugs are small beetles, usually only a quarter of an inch long. A female lays her little yellow eggs on a leaf. She lays hundreds of eggs—sometimes as many as a thousand.

The young hatch from the eggs in about five days. Like the young of most insects, they look very different from their parents. The young ladybugs look like little black-legged lizards. Their bodies are covered with spines and marked with bright colors such as orange or blue. They eat aphids just as the adults do. In three weeks they turn into pupae. They remain pupae for about a week, slowly changing into adults.

The pupal case finally breaks open. The ladybug is still light-colored, but soon its body begins to dry and harden and turns a brighter color. Then it flies off to look for aphids and other insects.

People who grow flowers or vegetables welcome ladybugs to their gardens. They usually wish that even more of these helpful beetles would come to feed on the pest insects that injure their plants. To supply this need, there are people who make a business of collecting ladybugs and selling them to farmers and gardeners.

One of the best places to collect ladybugs is California. Ladybugs often gather in large numbers to hibernate in the mountains. One collector found nearly 750 million ladybugs hi-

The ladybug beetle has been a friend to human beings for many centuries.

bernating on bushes in one small area of the mountains in California.

When ladybugs are collected in large numbers they are kept in refrigerators until spring. Then they are packed in straw and shipped to buyers all over the country. Farmers usually buy three thousand ladybugs for every acre they plan to farm.

Some people think that ladybugs are only valuable for controlling pests in small gardens. But this is not true. In some cases they have been more effective than pesticides in protecting crops over wide areas. The most famous case of this kind occurred over one hundred years ago when a scale insect threatened to destroy California's orange groves.

At that time, growers in California imported some orange trees from Australia. No one noticed that an insect called the cottony cushion scale arrived in this country clinging to the orange trees. Soon the larvae of the scale insects spread to other orange trees. Beetles and other creatures that often eat scale insects in this country had never seen cottony cushion scales and so they left them alone. The scale insects multiplied and spread. The orange growers realized that so many of their trees were dying that they might be put out of business.

The growers asked the government to help them find a way to get rid of the cottony cushion scale. The government sent a scientist to Australia to find out why those insects were not much of a pest there. This scientist did a little detective work. He found that there was a ladybug beetle in Australia that ate nothing but cottony cushion scales. This beetle ate so many scale insects that it kept their numbers down and people hardly even noticed them.

The scientist collected a large number of the ladybugs and shipped them to California. There they were turned loose in the orange groves, and within a year they had eaten almost all of the scale insects. The ladybug had saved California's orange groves.

The ladybug is everywhere in the meadow during summer. It comes to the milkweed plants to feed on the aphids and scale insects. It eats its own weight in insects every day.

A ladybug is fun to watch on a milkweed plant. It cleans itself as thoroughly as a cat. When a ladybug has finished a meal it puts its forelegs up to its mouth to clean them and then uses them to wash its face. It rubs its other legs rapidly together, cleaning them too. Then it flies off to another plant, looking for more aphids.

11. EGGS ON A LEAF

THE LEAVES OF THE milkweed plants are no longer clean and clear. Many have been chewed by caterpillars and beetles. Other leaves are blackened or withered where sucking insects have removed their juices. Some leaves have been stained by their own milky liquid where insects have cut into their veins. Here and there they are spotted by honeydew.

The most interesting spots of all may be overlooked. Perhaps partly hidden on the underside of a leaf are clusters of tiny objects. A close look shows that the objects in any one cluster are exactly alike because they are the eggs laid by an insect.

Some of the insects are mating and laying their eggs at this time. The males are courting females on warm summer days. In many cases they court their mates just as birds do, by song or color. Some scientists think that crickets chirp to find a

An insect has laid a cluster of eggs on a milkweed leaf.

mate. Male beetles display their bright colors to the females. Butterflies and moths often find their mates by the sense of smell.

Scientists are only just beginning to realize how important the sense of smell is for courting insects. Some insects manufacture substances known as pheromones. These chemicals give off distinct odors to other insects and serve as signals to them. Each kind of insect distributes a chemical whose odor is different from that of any other kind.

A female insect, for instance, may release a pheromone. Males of her kind are able to smell this chemical even a long distance away. Thus, the odor makes it easier for them to find a mate.

In the last chapter we saw that aphids are often produced without a father. But most insects, as humans do, need both a male and a female to produce their young. The eggs laid by the female will not produce living young unless they are fertilized by a male.

Female insects do not usually care for their eggs, unlike birds, after laying them. They leave them in a safe place and then fly away. Female insects have an egg-laying organ called an ovipositor. This is a tube which the female may use to pierce a plant or the ground and push in her eggs. Some wasps and other insects even use their ovipositor to lay their eggs inside the bodies of other insects. When the eggs hatch, the larvae begin feeding on this insect and finally kill it.

Insects lay eggs in many sizes and shapes. They may be so small that we cannot see them without a microscope. They may be round, or shaped like a cone, a barrel or a coin. Some may look like little acorns.

The monarch butterfly lays only one egg on a leaf. Most insects lay their eggs in clusters. Some insects make a cover or egg case to protect the eggs and then fasten it to the bark of a tree or some other sheltered place.

So the next time you handle a leaf, look closely at those little spots. They may be eggs containing the young insects that one day soon will be all around you in the meadow.

12. TRAVELING BAGS

THE MILKWEED HAS burst into bloom. Everywhere in the meadow the round little buds have sprung open, peeling back to reveal the flower inside. The air above the flowers is now a busy highway for honeybees. The bees, their hairy bodies gleaming bright gold in the sun, circle the flowers. They land on them, gather the pollen, and fly off toward the hive. Other honeybees fly into the meadow so that the hum never ceases.

Honeybees and other pollen-gathering insects are an important part of the milkweed's life. Without them the plant would flower uselessly. It would never be fertilized to produce new plants next summer. Honeybees are not like the aphids that suck a milkweed's juices and sometimes kill it. By coming to the flowers for nectar, the bees perform a valuable service for the entire milkweed colony.

Sometimes we like to think that a flower blooms only for our own pleasure. It is sweet-smelling and beautiful. But from the plant's point of view a flower blooms only to make another plant. It manufactures pollen that must be carried to another

There are at least fifty flowers in each cluster on the plant.

flower. When pollen reaches another flower we say that the flower is pollinated. Pollen fertilizes the flower and allows it to produce the seeds from which new plants will grow.

Milkweed flowers have a remarkable way of getting bees to pollinate them. They are colored a light pink or a pale lav-

The buds open to reveal five nectar-filled cups on every flower.

ender. There are at least fifty flowers in each cluster on the plant.

If you look at its picture you will see that a milkweed flower has five cups. Each cup is filled with nectar, the sweet liquid that bees come to gather for making honey. A milkweed's nectar is so thick and sweet that French-Canadians used to make brown sugar from it. They gathered the flowers in the early morning when they were still wet with dew, then boiled down the dew to produce the sugar.

A honeybee is attracted to a milkweed flower by its color and its sweet-smelling nectar. The bee lands on a flower. It is not easy for it to hold on. Its weight may bend the flower over. The flower itself is smooth and slippery. But the flower has several convenient places where a nectar-drinking insect can put its feet, and these places lead directly to the pollen.

Look at the picture again. Five little tongues reach out of the five nectar cups and rest on the center of the flower. Around the center, just below the top and between each two cups, are black dots. Below each dot is a slit in the center of the flower. As the bee bends to sip nectar from the cup, it keeps pumping its feet to keep its balance. One of its feet usually fits neatly into a slit between the cups.

Inside the opening where the bee has put its foot are two sticky bags which hold the yellow pollen. The bee keeps pumping its foot up and down. As its foot moves it splits the black dot at the top of the opening. The bee's foot gets stuck in this clamp.

The bee has finished drinking the cup's nectar. It is ready to leave but its foot is stuck tight in the clamp. It struggles to free itself. Sometimes smaller insects or even a bee are not able to pull their feet out and they die there on the flower. But a honeybee is usually strong enough to get free. As it pulls its foot out it also pulls out the clamp that is attached to the pollen bags. The bee flys away, carrying the pollen bags still stuck to its foot.

The bee flies to another flower. Once again it tries to keep its balance as it sips nectar from the cup. It pumps its foot up and down. A foot carrying the sticky pollen bags slips into the opening between the cups. When it finishes drinking, the bee must struggle once more to pull its foot from the clamp. It pulls itself free at last. But this time the pollen bags remain behind in the flower.

Between each cup there is a slit in the center of the flower. At the top of each slit there is a black dot.

A bee fly, its foot trapped, died on the flower.

Milkweed flowers are fragrant, but will die quickly if picked.

The honeybee has flown away, but it has already performed its service for the milkweed flower. Behind the opening where the pollen bags were left there is a liquid in which the pollen grains begin to grow. The grains send out tubes into the flower's pistil. The pollen tubes move down the pistil's stalk, until they reach the bottom of the flower where they touch the ovules.

Ovules are small grains which become seeds if they are fertilized. The pollen brought to this flower by the honeybee joins with the ovules to become seeds. The ovules have been fertilized.

Very few of the milkweed's flowers are fertilized. Every step in the process has to take place at the right time. The honeybee or other nectar-eating insect must go through all of the right steps, and it is often a matter of luck when it carries the pollen bags from one flower to another. Perhaps only one or two flowers out of the several hundred on each plant become fertilized and produce seeds. Seeds, like eggs, must be fertilized to produce young.

For the time being there is no way to tell which of the flowers holds developing seeds. The seeds develop deep in the flower where we don't see them. The unfertilized flowers look just as pretty and smell as sweet as the ones holding seeds.

When we see a pretty wild flower that is abundant we sometimes want to pick it and take it home with us. We think how pretty it will look in a jar with water. But we will be disappointed if we pick or cut the milkweed flowers. When the stem is broken the milky juice seeps out and soon hardens over the wound. It seals the tissues so that the stem can no longer take up water. The milkweed flower in our jar will quickly droop.

13. THE LIFE OF THE HONEY BEE

WHY DO HONEYBEES come to the milkweed flowers?

Honeybees live in a community called the hive. Those that come to the milkweed meadow are worker bees. It is their job to spend each day gathering honey or pollen and bringing it back to the hive for food.

Honeybees are not native to the United States. They were brought here by the early settlers. Indians called them "the white man's fly." Most honeybees still live in man-made hives, usually large wooden boxes divided into different areas for the bees' use. Some swarms of honeybees have escaped from man's care and live together inside hollow trees. As many as 80,000 bees may live together in a hive.

A hive has three kinds of bees. Each hive has a queen, a large bee whose constant duty is to lay eggs. She is a living egg factory. She may lay as many as 1,500 eggs a day. A hive also has a few male bees called drones whose only duty is to mate with the queen, fertilizing the eggs. Afterward the drones are killed by the worker bees, the third group. These small hairy bees are all females. As their name suggests, they do most of the work for the hive.

When the queen's eggs hatch, the baby bees are put in tiny cells made of beeswax. The workers bring back large amounts of nectar and pollen for the hungry babies. Other worker bees called nursemaids feed them. After six days the babies, or larvae, spin cocoons in their cells. They spend two weeks in the cocoons growing legs and wings. When they come out, they are worker bees themselves.

The young workers are well fitted for their job. They have strong wings. They have a little sack called a pollen basket on each hind leg. And they have a long tongue for sipping nectar from flowers.

Before they fly off in search of nectar or pollen, honeybees must make sure that they can find their way back to the hive. They fly around the outside of the hive and become familiar with the landmarks that will help them to find their way.

Honeybees often travel several miles to find flowers. They seem to be attracted to milkweed flowers more by their sweet odor than by their color. They come to milkweed only for nectar. They cannot use milkweed pollen because it is wrapped in the sticky pollen bags.

When honeybees find nectar they like, they collect only from that kind of flower. The bee that has made the discovery flies back to the hive. Scientists have learned that a bee is able to "tell" the other workers back at the hive all about her discovery.

The other workers know at once what kind of flower she has found because they can smell the nectar she has brought back. Then the worker goes into a curious dance. The signals she gives during the dance tell the workers the direction in which they must fly to find the nectar and how far away it is.

When the bees collect nectar they hold it in a part of the body called a crop. The nectar begins to turn into honey in the

A worker honeybee comes to the milkweed flower to gather nectar.

crop as the bees fly back to the hive. There they store the honey in cells where other workers refine it into pure honey.

It is a hard life for the worker bees. They fly so many miles a day that their wings begin to wear out. Their bright golden bodies turn a darker color. They usually die toward the end of summer after working for two months. The queen lives all winter to start a new colony the next year.

Fortunately for us the bees work so hard that they store more honey in the hive than they need. The men and women who keep honeybees are able to collect plenty of honey to sell to their customers.

"Our common milkweed is a major source of honey wherever it is abundant," says Dr. Francis O. Holmes, a scientist who keeps his own bees. "It is one of the best sources of nectar for honeybees. It is a light amber in color and it tastes as sweet as it smells."

14. SEE, HEAR, TOUCH AND SMELL

IT IS MIDSUMMER. Flowers bloom everywhere in the meadow, painting it in many colors. There are the pinks of wild roses, the bright yellows of St. Johnswort and the deep blue of cow vetch. As we run our hand across the plants we feel many textures—smooth leaves, hairy stems, prickly twigs.

The sweet smells of summer are all around us. The milkweed flowers put forth some of the sweetest. The grasses have a sweetness of their own. But not all the odors of the meadow are pleasant. Crouched on a milkweed leaf is an insect that is notorious for the bad smell it can give off. It is called the stinkbug.

The stinkbug, colored green and patterned like the leaf it sits on, is hard to see at first. But when we look closely we see a fierce-looking creature that looks as if it is wearing a suit of armor. Its bad smell comes from scent glands on its thorax. People say that if it gets on raspberry plants it gives the berries a bad taste.

The stinkbug, which can give off a bad odor, looks as if it wears a shield.

If we stop to listen for a moment we find that the summer meadow is almost as noisy as a busy town. The hum of honeybees seems to be everywhere. The hum comes from the bees' wings, which scientists have timed at two hundred beats a second. In contrast, a ladybug beats her wings only seventy-five times a second. Each kind of insect beats its wings at a different speed so that the meadow is filled with different levels of humming. Parts of their beating wings vibrate as they fly, producing a sound just as a tuning fork does when it is struck.

A field sparrow sings its sweet song from a bush at the edge of the meadow. A crow perches on one of the invading tree and calls, "Caw! Caw!" A goldfinch crosses the meadow in its lively bouncing flight and utters its chattering call that seems to say, "Potato-chip! Potato-chip!"

There are many sounds coming from the grass. The sounds are made by grasshoppers. Grasshoppers have short antennae and two pairs of short legs up front. But their hind legs are very long and powerful. Grasshoppers have to be able to jump a long distance to escape the birds that come to feed on them.

The grasshoppers use those huge legs as musical instruments too. Some grasshoppers make a soft, purring sound by rubbing their hind legs together. Other kinds rub one hind leg against the lower edge of a front wing to make a buzzing sound. Everyone who goes to the meadow hears sharp crackling noises around them in the tall grass. This sound is made by grasshoppers as they snap their hind wings in flight.

Life does not slow down in the meadow as the sun sets and evening comes on. Some flowers close, it is true, and some animals sleep. But other animals are stirring. From low bushes and plants come loud, insistent calls: "Katy-did! Katy-didn't!"

These loud calls are made by a long-horned grasshopper called the katydid. It is a green insect, patterned like the leaves it hides among, with long hairlike antennae. The antennae are longer than its body. Sometimes, as it feeds on leaves, it keeps one antenna pointed forward and the other backward. One naturalist has said that it is as if the insect is "on the lookout for news from the front and the rear."

The katydid calls to find a mate by rubbing its front wings together. One wing has a file on its edge and the other wing has a scraper. It makes a song by rubbing the scraper over the file. Some people think that the song is harsh when the insect is close, but it is more musical at a distance.

Katydids are hard to find because they look so much like a

The katydid has long legs and antennae. This young one has not yet grown wings.

part of a leaf. But if you take a flashlight into the meadow with you at dusk you can follow the song to find the singer. Katydids sing faster as the temperature rises. In fact, you can tell the temperature by how fast they are singing. Count the number of calls they make in a minute. Add 161 to the number of calls. Then divide the total by three. The figure you get will be the temperature.

Now the meadow is dark. The katydid calls from a milkweed plant. Suddenly, tiny yellow lights begin to flash over the meadow. Other lights flash as if in answer. These lights are the signals sent out by fireflies as they hunt for mates.

Fireflies are beetles that have tail-lights at the tip of their abdomens. They can turn their lights on and off like an electric bulb. Scientists say they give off a cold light—if you hold a beetle in your hand, you feel no heat when it flashes its light.

Each kind of firefly flashes its light differently. Experts can tell one kind from another just by seeing how many flashes are sent out and how long there is between flashes. When a female firefly sees a male of her own kind flashing, she lights up in answer. The male sees her signal and he comes to find her.

Young fireflies and some females have no wings or flashing lights. But their tails have a greenish glow. They are called glowworms. The female of one kind of firefly not only can flash a light but she can imitate the flashes sent out by the females of other kinds. The males of those other kinds of fireflies come looking for her. She pounces on them and eats them!

Even at night the meadow goes on changing energy from one form to another. Insects and other animals feed on the plants. Predators feed on the plant-eating animals. Plants and animals die and decay, enriching the soil. When morning comes the meadow is a different place than it was before.

15. BUTTERFLIES AND A MOTH

THE ANIMALS THAT may account for the greatest turnover of energy in the meadow are the moths and butterflies. We can find their caterpillars on almost every plant, endlessly chewing up green leaves. They change these leaves to their own body tissues as they rapidly grow. Their bodies, in turn, are changed into food for the many creatures, from tiny wasps to large birds, that hunt them in the meadow.

Moths and butterflies belong to the second largest order of insects, just behind the beetles. There are 100,000 different kinds. They are called *lepidoptera,* which means "scaly-winged."

Butterflies are sometimes called "flowers that fly." As they flutter from flower to flower, they add great color and beauty to the meadow. Strangely enough, the wings themselves are colorless. It is the scales that give them some of the most fascinating color combinations in nature.

A monarch butterfly has taste buds on its feet. When it tastes nectar the long tongue automatically unrolls into the flower.

Scales are very tiny dustlike plates that overlap like shingles on a butterfly's wings. As they overlap, the scales fit together to form the marvelous patterns of color and design that we see.

Butterflies fly during the day. Some kinds fly only when the sun shines. They come to flowers to sip nectar. Their bodies carry pollen from one flower to another. Aside from bees, the butterflies and moths pollinate more flowers than any other insects.

Butterflies are attracted to brightly colored flowers, especially ones that have red or pink in their petals. Many of these

The blue swallowtail butterfly has tail-like tips on its wings.

flowers close up at night. A butterfly always lands on a flower to sip it. It lifts its wings, holding them upright over its back.

A butterfly has taste buds on its feet. Scientists say that these organs can taste the tiniest hint of sugar in water and are two thousand times as sensitive as a human being's. If a butterfly's feet taste nectar on a flower, its long hollow tongue

Toward the end of summer the wings of the tiger swallowtail butterfly become worn and tattered.

unrolls at once. The butterfly pushes it into the flower and sucks the nectar as through a straw.

The monarch butterfly is the most familiar in the milkweed meadow. Nearly as abundant are the big swallowtail butterflies that also come to sip nectar from milkweeds. They get their names from the tail-like points on each wing. Tiger swallowtails are marked with black and yellow stripes and their wings measure five inches across. Blue swallowtails have shiny blue-green wings with small white spots.

These butterflies lay their eggs in the meadow. The eggs hatch into caterpillars. The caterpillars spend all their time with their heads pressed down to the leaves, chewing as fast as they can. They do not have to see very well. Each has a row of tiny simple eyes on both sides of its head that can do little more than tell light from dark.

Most caterpillars spin out a silken thread beneath them as they crawl along a leaf. The silk is made from two different kinds of liquid that come out of the lower lip and harden together as they reach the air. The caterpillars use the thread to help them hold onto the slippery leaf, just as we might hold onto a rail along a narrow walk. If something bothers the caterpillar, it may simply roll off the leaf and dangle in midair by the thread.

The caterpillar of the tiger swallowtail puts its silk to good use. It spins a tight web across a curled leaf. Then it uses the web as a hammock to rest on when it is not feeding. Many kinds of swallowtail caterpillars have big round spots on their thoraxes that look just like eyes. If a bird swoops down to eat the caterpillar it is often frightened away by the "eyes," which make the caterpillar look like the head of a huge snake.

Butterflies usually spend the winter as either caterpillars or pupae. Most butterflies do not make a cocoon when they pupate. The caterpillar changes into a curious-looking object called a chrysalis. The chrysalis of the monarch butterfly is a beautiful shade of green with gold spots—people call it "the emerald house with golden nails." Those of many swallowtails look like green leaves, hung in a safe place by a thread of silk.

The lives of adult butterflies are very different from those of hungry caterpillars. Some butterflies never eat at all. The others lead a lazy life, drifting over the meadow and sometimes stopping at a flower to sip a little nectar. Their chief business is to mate and lay eggs. Toward the end of summer the wings of most butterflies become torn and tattered. They are ready to

The hummingbird moth hovers before flowers and sips nectar through its long hollow tongue. Its beating wings are a blur.

die. For some monarchs, as we shall see, the story takes another course.

The hummingbird moth visits the milkweed meadow with the butterflies. Most moths come at night, but the hummingbird moth flies by day. It gets its name from the fact that it does not land on flowers as butterflies do, but hovers in front of them like a hummingbird. It is able to feed on nectar without landing because it has a long, hollow tongue. Sometimes it carries away milkweed pollen bags stuck to its tongue by accident.

When the hummingbird moth feeds in front of a flower its rapidly beating wings seem to be just a blur. This insect is able to fly at high speed. It is sometimes called the clear-winged moth because it lacks scales over much of its wings and they are transparent. At rest its chunky hairy body makes the hummingbird moth look like the bumblebee.

16. ONE PLANT, FOUR VEGETABLES

THE MILKWEED FLOWERS are beginning to fade. But deep in the flowers there is still much going on. The pollen grains carried from one flower to another by insects have fertilized the ovules. The ovules have ripened into seeds. The ovary holding the seeds is turning into a pod. Milkweed pods perform the same service that pea pods do, forming a case to hold the seeds.

The young milkweed pod is soft, green and velvety. This is the season of the year when native Americans gathered the pods for food. White travelers to Indian villages reported that there were often milkweed patches near the wigwams. The Indians knew what many other Americans are finding out today. People who know about milkweed agree with the early Indians that this plant is one of the best vegetables that nature offers us.

Milkweed flowers' ovaries ripen into seed pods.

These people do not consider milkweed to be a "weed." If there is none growing wild near their homes, they plant milkweed at the edge of their gardens. It is easy to care for. It does not have to be fertilized and weeded like garden crops. As it grows, it provides four different kinds of vegetables.

Its value as a vegetable is one of the many curious things about milkweed. It gives plant-eating insects a bad taste. Cows and other grazing animals don't like to eat milkweed. But when the different parts of the plant are very young and tender the bitter taste is absent.

People who like to eat milkweed begin watching the plants as soon as they poke their tips above ground in the spring. As each part of the milkweed becomes ready, it is picked and carried away to the kitchen.

The first part of the plants that appear are the shoots in spring. They are light green and tender. When they are five or six inches tall people cut them off with a knife, tie them in little bunches and cook them like asparagus. This is the time of year when green vegetables are most appreciated because the garden plants are not yet ready. Later on the shoots grow taller and become too tough to eat.

From the shoots the tiny green leaves begin to unfold. The ones at the top of the plant are tender and delicious. If they are picked early enough, they are not yet bitter and can be eaten raw in salads. The leaves can also be cooked like spinach.

The weeks pass. Caterpillars have chewed the leaves, aphids have sucked the juices and the sun beats down on the meadow. The milkweeds keep on growing. Soon the clusters of tightly packed buds appear on the plants. The milkweed watchers return to the plant to gather the bud clusters. They steam them and serve them like broccoli, which is another plant whose buds we eat.

The buds that remain on the plants open into flowers. The bees, which come to the flowers for nectar, also help to fertilize their seeds. The pods begin to form around the seeds. When these pods become about an inch long, they are light green and soft. Many people think the pod is the tastiest part of the plant. They like the nutty taste that the tiny immature seeds give to this vegetable. They are especially good when they are french fried.

The reason that all these parts of the milkweed are tasty is that they are picked when they are young and very tender. They become bitter only with age. But milkweed's value as a food plant does not end with the four parts just described. The

Some people steam and eat milkweed bud clusters like broccoli.

honey that bees make from milkweed nectar would make the plant special even if it had no other uses.

For hundreds of years, people on several continents thought of milkweed as a medicine. The scientific name for the milkweed family is Asclepias, which refers to the ancient Greek god of medicine, Asclepius. The Indians and early white settlers boiled the powdered milkweed root and used it as a kind of laxative. Milkweed was listed by the U. S. Government until 1882 as a drug to treat ailments such as gallstones.

The milkweed is a nice plant to have near us even if we do not think of it as a vegetable. Some people plant it in their flower gardens. The flowers are beautiful and sweet smelling. They attract colorful and interesting insects, such as butterflies and moths. In one form or another milkweed grows throughout most of our country.

That is why some people say that the milkweed should be our national flower.

17. SPIDERS

IF A VISITOR COMES to the meadow early in the morning he or she will learn things that would not be possible later in the day. Only the visitor who comes early will realize how many spiders live in the meadow. When the dew still covers the ground, the strands of all the spider webs glisten with tiny beads of dew. Then they are easy to see.

Spiders play an important part in the life of the meadow. They eat many kinds of insects and keep them from becoming too numerous. Other insects, such as wasps, are able to live and raise their young by feeding on spiders.

There is a spider on a milkweed leaf. It is waiting for an insect to pass so that it can catch it. It is a crab spider. Like other spiders, it has eight legs. It gets its name because it runs sideways—even backwards—on its long legs.

A funnel spider waits for an insect to become trapped in its web.

The crab spider does not a spin a web as most other spiders do. It sits and waits for insects to pass. During the peak of the summer, when many flowers are in bloom, it catches many insects. It sometimes hides inside the flowers and catches flies or even honeybees which come for pollen. Although it is smaller than some of these insects, it is very fierce and quickly kills

The crab spider walks sideways and even backwards like a crab. It sometimes kills insects larger than itself.

Many people are afraid of spiders, but usually they will not hurt us if we handle them carefully.

One of the most beautiful spiders in the meadow is the orb-weaver, here resting head downward in its web.

them. It sucks the juices out of their bodies and then drops them in a pile on the ground beneath its hiding place.

Spiders differ from insects in many ways. Besides having eight legs, their bodies have two regions instead of three. The head and the thorax are combined into one part and contain the spider's eyes, mouth and legs. The abdomen contains many other organs, including the spinnerets. These are the tools by which it spins its silk.

Spiders don't go through the many changes or metamorphoses that we find in insects. The female spider, which is usually larger than the male, wraps her eggs in a silk sac. When the young hatch from the eggs they look just like little adult spiders.

Many kinds of spiders in the meadow spin webs. Some of them are called funnel-weaving spiders. They make webs that look like funnels in the grass or on leaves. The spider hides in the funnel-like structure. When an insect is caught in the web the spider comes out and captures it.

The most beautiful spiders in the meadow are the orb-weaving spiders. Some of them are colored a pale yellow with black stripes. Many people are afraid of spiders, but ordinarily they will not hurt us if we handle them carefully. We can admire the beauty of the orb-weaving spider and the large round webs it makes.

These spiders spin webs that are like works of art. We often see the orb-weaver, resting head downward in the middle of the web. The strands of its web that radiate outward are made of simple silk, but those that spiral around the web are sticky.

Spiders do not have wings but young spiders can "fly." Late in the summer when the young have hatched they move to other parts of the countryside. The young spiders get up on a rock or a post and start spinning a long thread. This silky thread is called gossamer. When the wind comes along it lifts the thread and the little spider attached to it high in the air. Like milkweed seeds, the little spiders are often carried miles away.

On days when the little spiders are traveling, the air is filled with gossamer.

18. THE FLIGHT OF THE MONARCHS

THE MONTHS OF SUMMER have been peaceful for the monarch butterflies in the milkweed meadow. Once in a while they sipped nectar from the flowers. They rested on the plants or flew from one to the other. Monarchs came together briefly during the mating season. At that time, the females were attracted to the males by the small pockets of perfume on the males' wings.

Now as autumn came on the monarch butterflies gathered again. Many other kinds of butterflies were dying. Other insects were going into hiding for the winter. But the monarchs, like many birds, were getting ready to fly south. These butterflies are among the very few insects that migrate in winter.

Monarch butterflies mate in the meadow.

The monarchs' strong wings, which are three or four inches across, carry them amazing distances. These butterflies have flown across oceans to start colonies in Australia and the Philippine Islands. They gather into flocks like birds. They begin to fly south. As they go they are joined by other flocks of monarchs.

In some years the monarchs are scarce. There is a virus disease that spreads through their population and kills many of them. But after two or three years the monarchs become numerous again. Sometimes in the autumn they travel south in flocks of thousands.

None of the insects have ever been south before because they live less than a year. But all of them seem to know the way. Some scientists think that they find their way by following the sun. When night comes, all of the flocks fly into a large tree to rest. The flocks all seem to choose the same trees along the way. Perhaps they smell traces of the other flocks that went ahead of them. Scientists say there is usually a milkweed meadow near the tree where they rest.

How do we know so much about the monarchs' migration? Much of our information comes from a program started in the 1930s by Dr. Fred Urquhart of the University of Toronto and his wife, Nora. They decided to catch monarchs before they left for the south and put little tags on their wings.

These tags are half the size of an ordinary postage stamp. One side has an adhesive that sticks to a monarch's wing. The outer side contains mailing instructions. The little tags do not interfere with the butterflies' flight.

The Urquharts spent many years making their program a success. They worked hard, tagging butterflies on their vacations. Their students helped them. In recent years hundreds of people have helped them tag butterflies or reported finding the tagged butterflies in the south. When people send back the tags they find on butterflies, the Urquharts can tell just where the monarch was tagged and where it was found. Each report fits another piece into place in the great puzzle of the monarch's migration.

Some monarchs fly all the way from Ontario, Canada, to central Mexico. That is a distance of 1,800 miles or more. As Nora Urquhart says, "A butterfly which makes that trip probably flies three times that distance because of all the detours it takes."

The monarch that leaves the milkweed meadow in the autumn never returns. It dies before the next summer. Its life span is nine months or less. The monarchs that fly back to the north in the spring are young ones that hatched in the south or somewhere along the return migration route.

19. MILKWEED SILK

THE MILKWEED FLOWERS have died. Many of the leaves have dropped off the plants. All over the meadow the milkweed plants are bursting into clumps of satiny white fluff.

The milkweed has gone to seed. The pods have grown and toughened, turning their tips toward the sky. The greenish-white pods are covered all over with little points or spines. In the western United States the spines are usually larger than those on the smoother pods that grow in the East. The pods are lined with seams.

Only the fertilized flowers produce pods. The seeds have developed inside them. Each pod begins to split along a seam, revealing the seeds. There are hundreds of brown seeds, over-lapping each other, packed into a pod.

The milkweed pods, their tips turned toward the sky, have burst open.

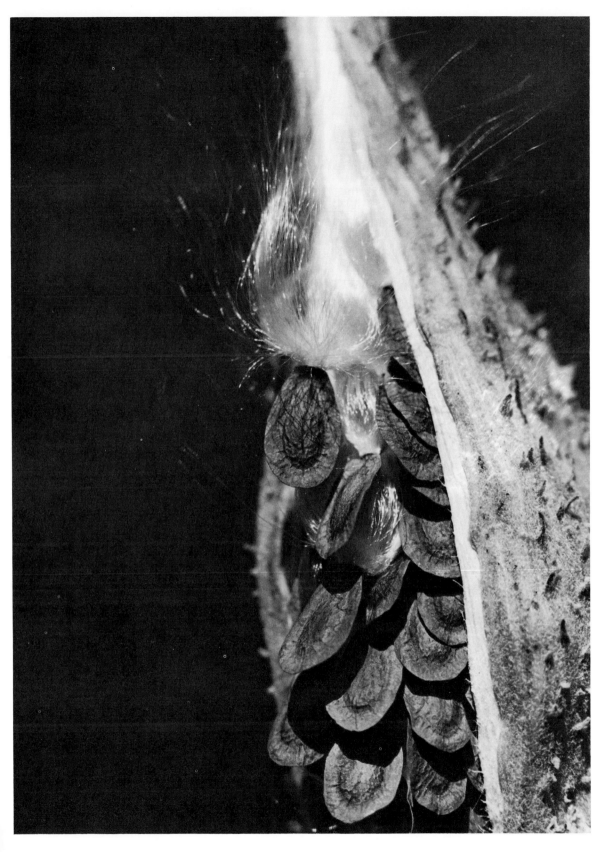

Hundreds of brown seeds are packed into each pod. Each seed is surrounded by a thin rim that serves as a "life preserver."

To each seed is attached a group of long white, silky hairs. Some scientists have counted them. They found about nine hundred hairs to a seed. Each hair is hollow and is coated with wax to keep out water. The hairs fluff out to form a little parachute. When the wind blows past the plants it pulls the seeds from the pods. The seeds rise on their parachutes and are carried away by the wind.

The parachutes allow milkweeds to spread over much of the country. Sometimes the seeds drift for miles on the wind. Each seed has a thin rim that is like cork. If it drops into the water, this "life preserver" keeps it afloat.

If you look into one of the pods, you may see a bright red-and-black-spotted insect called the milkweed bug. This is one of the seed bugs. It feeds on the seeds. Some scientists have seen these bugs lifted right out of the pod on a seed by the wind. Then it goes on a free parachute ride to another meadow!

The milkweed bug has sucking mouth parts. Its beak has two separate tubes that let it "drink" solid food. The bug fastens its beak to a milkweed seed. Through one tube it pumps saliva into the seed. The saliva contains a chemical that dissolves the inside of the seed to a liquid. The bug sucks up the liquid through the other tube. Then, as one scientist writes, "the bug is full and the seed is empty."

Goldfinches and other birds come to the meadow for the seeds too. They crush them and feed them to their young. The seeds are rich in oil, and some people press them to make a cooking oil.

For a long time the silk attached to the seeds has been used by human beings. The settlers used it to stuff mattresses and pillows. They also mixed it with wool or flax for spinning, though the weak, brittle hairs are not well suited for this. During World War II, the silky hairs played a part in America's war effort.

The Navy needed thousands of life jackets in case ships were sunk or planes shot down into the sea. Life jackets keep people from drowning because they are stuffed with light mate-

The seed's silky hairs fluff out to form a parachute.

rial that floats. They are usually stuffed with kapok, which comes from trees in the East Indies. Kapok supplies were cut off from the United States by the war.

There are no trees in the United States that provide a light, corky material like kapok. Then scientists remembered

Children in many states collected milkweed silk during World War II to stuff life jackets.

milkweed hairs, which are light and resist water. The government started a program, asking children to collect milkweed pods. Farmers were given seed and were paid to plant milkweed so that there would be more pods available.

Children in many states collected milkweed pods. They took the silky hairs off the seeds and stuffed them into onion bags that the government provided. Then the children hung up

The milkweed bug enters a pod looking for seeds to "drink."

Milkweed seeds drift off on the wind, perhaps to create a new colony.

the bags to dry the silk. The government paid them twenty cents a bag, which was a fair price at that time.

Many children worked hard to supply this valuable material. In 1944 they collected 150,000 pounds of silk. It was taken to a factory in Petoskey, Michigan, where the silk was processed. Then it was made into life jackets or a lining for flying suits. Two or three pounds of milkweed silk in a life jacket kept a man afloat for three days.

After the war, the milkweed silk became too expensive to collect in large amounts. There is no machine that can harvest it cheaply. But children still love to collect and open a few pods. As they blow into the pods the light and airy seeds drift off on the wind, creating patterns in the air.

20. THE BROKEN POD

THE MEADOW IS DESERTED. It lies under patches of snow. The brown stems of last year's milkweed plants seem to shiver and rattle in the cold northern wind.

The part of the milkweed above ground has died. But under the frozen ground, perhaps as deep as seven feet, the tap root of the milkweed clump is only sleeping. If we could look underground we would see that all of the plants in the milkweed patch are connected by a complicated system of roots. The milkweed patch is really one huge plant. Each of the stems that we see in summer is only a part of the whole.

Winter is not harmful to the milkweed patch. In fact, if it were not exposed to wintry cold, the patch would not grow again in the spring. It needs a period of cold to rest and

become strong again. Milkweed patches are usually largest in the northern part of the country.

Much of the energy that was exchanged through the meadow during the summer is stored for the winter. The plants and animals that died have decayed into the soil and enriched it for another year. They have left behind them the seeds and eggs that are packages of sleeping energy, ready to refuel the cycle of life in the world of the milkweed in the first warm days of spring.

ADA and FRANK GRAHAM have long been active in the fields of ecology and conservation. They live in Milbridge, Maine. Frank Graham is a Field Editor of *Audubon* Magazine and has written a number of popular books, including *Since Silent Spring* and *Gulls: A Social History*. Ada Graham directs an outdoor nature program for school children. Together the Grahams have written more than a dozen books for young readers, including *The Mystery of the Everglades, The Careless Animal, Dooryard Garden and the Golden/Audubon Primers*.

LES LINE is a well-known photographer and the editor of *Audubon*. His wildlife photographs have appeared in many publications. The pictures in this book were taken at an Audubon Sanctuary in Sharon, Connecticut. Mr. Line lives in Dobbs Ferry, New York.